This book belongs to:

Sophia

for Thomas and Anna

LIBRARY OF CONGRESS CATALOGING-IN-PUBLICATION DATA

Bates, Ivan. Five little ducks / illustrated by Ivan Bates. p. cm. "Orchard Book." Summary: One by one,
five little ducks wander away from their mother until her lonely quack brings them all waddling back.
ISBN 0-439-74693-0 • 1. Nursery rhymes. 2. Children's poetry. [1. Nursery rhymes. 2. Ducks—
Poetry. 3. Counting.] I. Title. PZ8.3.B3185Fiv 2006 [E]—dc22   2005000112

10 9 8 7 6 5 4 3 2 1   06 07 08 09 10 • Printed in Singapore   46

Reinforced Binding for Library Use • First edition, February 2006

The illustrations for this book were done in colored pencil and watercolor
on Arches paper. The text type was set in Poliphilus MT Regular.
The display type was set in Script MT.

Book design by Alison Klapthor

Five Little Ducks

Illustrated by IVAN BATES

Orchard Books ❉ New York
An imprint of Scholastic Inc.

*F*ive little ducks
Went out one day
Over the hills and far away.
Mother duck said,
"Quack, quack, quack."

But only four little ducks
came waddling back.

Four little ducks
Went out one day
Over the hills and far away.
Mother duck said,
"Quack, quack, quack."

But only three little ducks
came waddling back.

Three little ducks
Went out one day
Over the hills and far away.
Mother duck said,
"Quack, quack, quack."

But only two little ducks
came waddling back.

Two little ducks
Went out one day
Over the hills and far away.
Mother duck said,
"Quack, quack, quack."

But only one little duck
came waddling back.

One little duck
Went out one day
Over the hills and far away.
Mother duck said,
"Quack, quack, quack."

But no little ducks
came waddling back.

Sad mother duck
Went out one day
Over the hills and far away.
Mother duck cried,
"Quack, quack, quack."

And all five little ducks
came waddling back!

Five Little Ducks

Brightly

Repeat melody for each verse

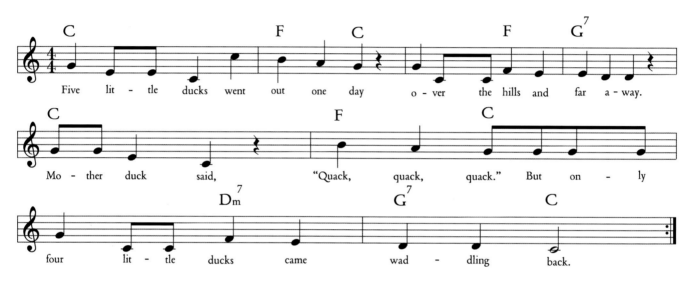

C F C F G⁷

Five lit – tle ducks went out one day o – ver the hills and far a – way.

C F C

Mo – ther duck said, "Quack, quack, quack." But on – ly

Dm⁷ G⁷ C

four lit – tle ducks came wad – dling back.

Verse 2

Four little ducks
Went out one day
Over the hills and far away.
Mother duck said,
"Quack, quack, quack."
But only three little ducks
came waddling back.

Verse 3

Three little ducks
Went out one day
Over the hills and far away.
Mother duck said,
"Quack, quack, quack."
But only two little ducks
came waddling back.

Verse 4

Two little ducks
Went out one day
Over the hills and far away.
Mother duck said,
"Quack, quack, quack."
But only one little duck
came waddling back.

Verse 5

One little duck
Went out one day
Over the hills and far away.
Mother duck said,
"Quack, quack, quack."
But no little ducks
came waddling back.

Verse 6

Sad mother duck
Went out one day
Over the hills and far away.
Mother duck cried,
"Quack, quack, quack."
And all five little ducks
came waddling back!